Being a valiant luchadora is a tradition in Lucía's family.
As Abu says, a luchadora is more than a masked wrestler
with swift moves, more than just a superhero with slick style.

A luchadora has moxie. She is brave and full of heart,
and isn't afraid to fight for what is right.

Sometimes, though, even luchadoras have to deal
with pesky little sisters…

LUCÍA the LUCHADORA and the MILLION + MASKS

BY: CYNTHIA LEONOR GARZA

POW!

Brooklyn, NY

ILLUSTRATED BY: ALYSSA BERMUDEZ

I bolt through the backyard in my silver cape and mask, my little sister Gemma crashing after me like thunder.

She goes CRACK

She goes CRUNCH

I leap from the tree house, my landing full of pizzazz.

Gemma jumps, too.

BUMBLE

TUMBLE

SPLAT

I put
my mask
down.

When
I look back,

POOF

it's gone.

I am
gobsmacked.

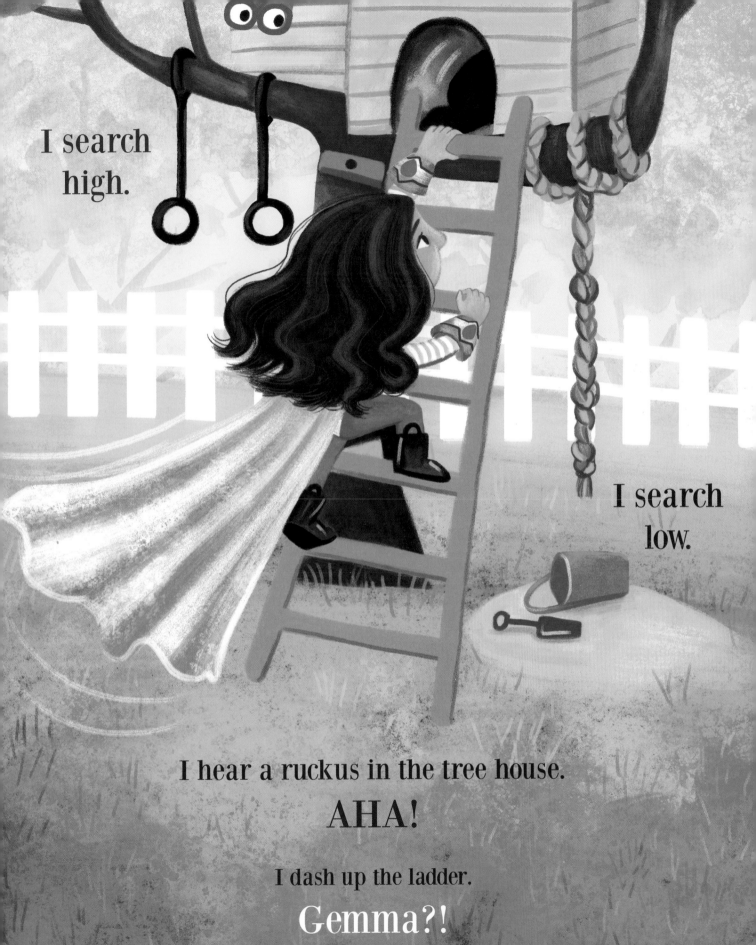

I search high.

I search low.

I hear a ruckus in the tree house.
AHA!

I dash up the ladder.
Gemma?!

My little sister has made **a ginormous hole** in my mask!

RIIIIIP

I rush to tell Abu about this terrible injustice.
This is **not right**, and I must fight for what is right,
like a real luchadora! **KA-POW!**

"What Gemma did was not right," Abu says.
"But she wants to be **a luchadora**, like you.
Gemma is just ... quixotic."

I bet
quixotic means
terrible.

"Gemma likes adventure," Abu says.

"She always finds trouble," I say.

HUFF! I feel exasperated.
Little sisters get away
with everything!
I will never
win.

"It is not always about
winning or losing," Abu says.
"Remember, the best adventures are shared."

Abu stitches my mask back up. Gemma says she's sorry.
Then, Abu tells us she has an idea.

The next day,
Abu takes me and
Gemma to a place
we've never been:
a mercado.

It's a market, but
it is not at all like
a supermarket.

It's more like
a *splendiferousmarket!*

Gemma's lips go SMACK when she sees
the cart piled with candied fruits.
My heart goes BIDI-BIDI when I hear the music.

There it is! The stand with **all the lucha libre masks!**
It'll be impossible to pick just one.

Abu tells us that one of the best luchadores of all time,
Mil Máscaras, wore a different mask every time he went into the ring.

Mil Máscaras! I could never keep track of a million masks.

Abu smiles. She tells me *mil* mean *one thousand*, not one million.

Mil Máscaras was known as the Man of a Thousand Masks.

PHEW!
One thousand is totally reasonable.

I can't wait to try them all on,
but Abu reminds me,
we're here to find a mask for Gemma.

HMPH.

Maybe with her own mask, Gemma will finally act like **a *real* luchadora.**

Maybe she'll stop finding **trouble.**

We get to work trying to find the right look for Gemma.

Too funky.

Too frightful.

UY

Too frou-frou.

JAJA

Too funny!

KERPLUNK

The lucha masks are all so different,
but marvelous! I take out my silver mask and slip it on.

I look at myself in the mirror …
and my heart goes KERPLUNK.

My mended mask doesn't feel so mighty anymore. Suddenly, my treasured mask seems so *tattered*.

I have a secret:
I wish I was

the **Girl** of a **Thousand Masks.**

If I had a thousand, or a *million* masks, I could become
a different luchadora Every! Single! Day!
I could *really* become ANYTHING
I dreamed of being.

I can't resist. I take off my mask and try on a new one.

Then another.

And another.

I feel a ZING run through me!

Gemma slips on a mask.

I look at the jumble of masks.
I still secretly want them all.

When I turn around, I spot
Gemma scampering off.

Oh no! I have to catch up
to her before she finds
trouble!

I slip on my mask.

I dash past the popsicle cart.
Gemma darts through the musicians.

I dodge a piñata.
Gemma ducks into a corner.

I've got her now.
She pounces, and finally,
I see what she's after.

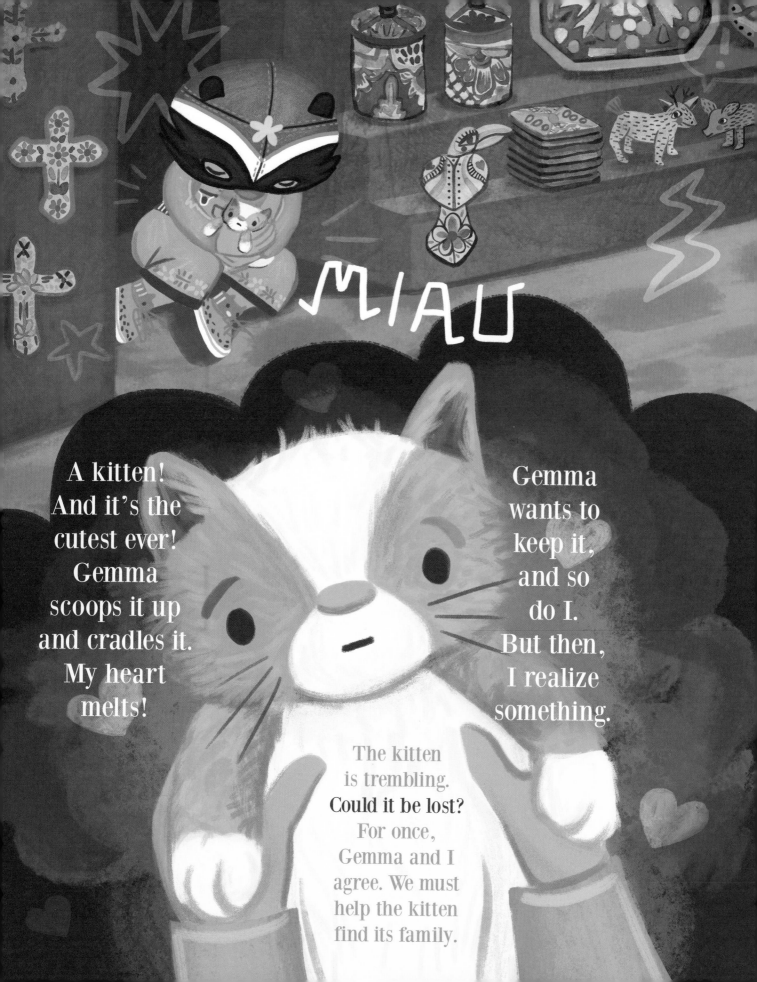

MIAU

A kitten!
And it's the
cutest ever!
Gemma
scoops it up
and cradles it.
My heart
melts!

Gemma
wants to
keep it,
and so
do I.
But then,
I realize
something.

The kitten
is trembling.
Could it be lost?
For once,
Gemma and I
agree. We must
help the kitten
find its family.

We ZIGZAG through the mercado with the kitten, searching.

When the candy lady sees us with the kitten, she points beneath a table.

MIAU,
MEOW,
MIAU, MEOW,
MIAU

A basket full of kittens! Now *this* is the cutest ever! It's a happy reunion.

Gemma and I high five. Then, we slink back to Abu. She is sealing the deal.

I take off my mask, and that's when
I realize something awful:

THIS IS NOT *MY* SILVER MASK!

My mask is missing, *again!*

Gemma rushes to help.
We search high. We search low.

Gemma pulls out a silver mask
from the pile, but it is not mine.
She hands me another.
Nope, not it.

We dig through
the entire pile of masks.
"Maybe you can get
a new mask," Gemma says.
"Or, you can have mine."

I know she
really means it,
but my heart goes

SNAP!

Even a thousand,
or a *million masks*
could never replace
my special
silver mask.
I sink to
the ground.

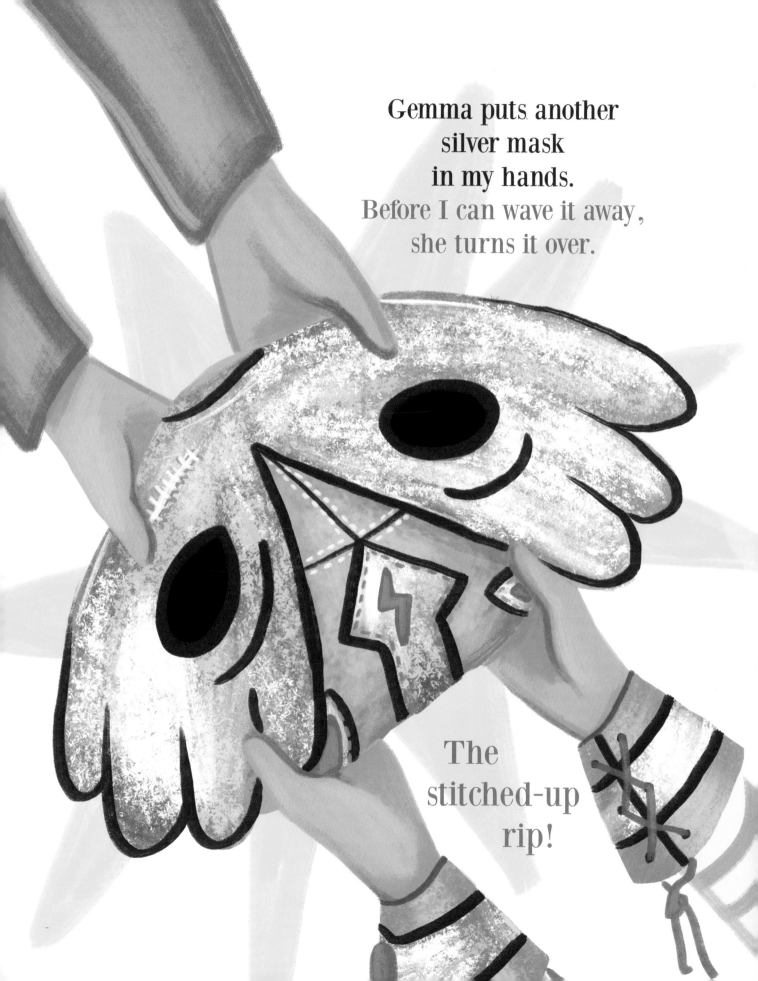

Gemma puts another
silver mask
in my hands.
Before I can wave it away,
she turns it over.

The
stitched-up
rip!

I dance. I prance.
I squeeze my marvelous mended mask!

Abu's mask. My mask.

I squeeze Gemma.

Maybe being quixotic
isn't always terrible.

Gemma is definitely One in a Million.

For my mother, Leonor - C.L.G. • To my Abuela, Lydia - A.B.

Lucía the Luchadora and the Million Masks

Text © 2018 Cynthia Leonor Garza
Illustrations © 2018 Alyssa Bermudez

Published by POW!
a division of powerHouse Packaging & Supply, Inc.
32 Adams Street, Brooklyn, NY 11201-1021

info@powkidsbooks.com
www.powkidsbooks.com

www.powerHouseBooks.com
www.powerHousePackaging.com

Library of Congress Control Number: 2018944213

ISBN: 978-1-57687-894-1

Printing and binding by Asia Pacific Offset.

Book design: Krzysztof Poluchowicz

10 9 8 7 6 5 4 3 2

Printed in China